Nat the Cat

by Miriam Sklar

ISBN: 978-1-338-75080-5
Illustrated by John Lund

Published by Scholastic Inc., 557 Broadway, New York, NY 10012

10 9 8 7 6 5 4 68 25 26 27/0

Printed in Jiaxing, China. First printing, January 2021.

Nat the cat likes to play.

Nat the cat likes to slide.

Nat the cat likes to climb.

Nat the cat likes to ride.

Nat the cat likes to leap.

Nat the cat likes to roll.

Nat the cat likes to sleep.